Withdrawn

DALE JARRETT: It Was Worth the Wait

BY JIM GIGLIOTTI

TRADITION BOOKS™
EXCELSIOR, MINNESOTA

Published by **Tradition Books**™ and distributed to the
school and library market by **The Child's World**®
P.O. Box 326
Chanhassen, MN 55317-0326
800/599-READ
http://www.childsworld.com

Photo Credits
Cover and title page: Allsport/Jonathan Ferrey (top); 5 Sports Gallery/
  Al Messerschmidt (bottom)
Allsport: 9 (Jamie Squire); 17 (Bill Hall)
AP/Wide World: 7, 8, 16, 24, 25, 30
Ken Coles: 12
Sports Gallery: 4 (Joe Robbins); 5 (Al Messerschmidt); 14, 18, 26, 28 (Brian Spurlock);
  21 (Brian Cleary); 22 (Tom Riles)

Book production by Shoreline Publishing Group, LLC
Art direction and design by The Design Lab

Library of Congress Cataloging-in-Publication Data
Gigliotti, Jim.
  Dale Jarrett : it was worth the wait / by Jim Gigliotti.
    p. cm. — (The world of NASCAR series)
Includes bibliographical references (p.) and index.
  ISBN 1-59187-002-X (lib. bdg. : alk. paper)
  1. Jarrett, Dale, 1956– —Juvenile literature. 2. Automobile racing drivers—United States—
Biography—Juvenile literature. [1. Jarrett, Dale, 1956– 2. Automobile racing drivers.] I. Title.
II. Series.
  GV1032.J37 G54 2002
  796.72'092—dc21   2002004641

Printed in the United States of America.

D A L E   J A R R E T T

Table of Contents

INTRODUCTION

A Long Time Coming

At an awards ceremony after the 2001 **NASCAR** season, Dale Jarrett was handed a check for his winnings. On the envelope containing the check, someone had written, "We want you to drive the truck."

Jarrett won the money driving a stock car, not a truck. The note referred to a funny advertisement for the United Parcel Service (UPS). The package delivery company sponsored Jarrett's number 88 white Ford Taurus prior to the 2001 racing season. The theme of the ads was to get Jarrett to race a big, brown UPS delivery truck, instead of his Ford Taurus.

"My part in the commercials is trying not to smile

Dale Jarrett can smile now, but his success in
NASCAR came after years of struggle.

and laugh much," Dale told NASCAR.com. "We have a lot of tapes that ended up on the floor because I couldn't keep a straight face."

The idea is all in fun, of course. Because of the ads, however, Jarrett became known around the country even by nonracing fans. It wasn't long ago that even the most devoted NASCAR fans didn't recognize Jarrett. Today, however, they all know that Dale Jarrett is one of the hottest drivers on the circuit.

Some of today's best racers, such as four-time **Winston Cup** champion Jeff Gordon, practically grew up inside of a race car. These drivers hit the ground running—often ahead of the pack—when they joined NASCAR. Jarrett's road to stardom took quite a bit longer.

"I hope our story is a little bit of an inspiration to others," Dale says.

Dale's No. 88 car sports the brown-and-white colors of his sponsor, UPS.

C H A P T E R   O N E

Like Father, Like Son

Dale Jarrett is the son of Ned Jarrett. Ned was a two-time NASCAR national champion in the 1960s. He's also a member of the International Motorsports Hall of Fame.

The elder Jarrett was called "Gentlemen Ned" when he was racing. Ned's pleasant demeanor hid a fierce competitiveness that helped him to 50 victories. In 1965, Ned captured his second national championship by winning 13 races and finishing among the top five in 42 events.

Ned and his wife, Martha, had three children—sons Glenn and Dale and daughter Patti. The kids grew up watching their father race around the tracks of North Carolina, but Dale was captivated by almost all sports. He was a talented baseball player as a youngster. He later became an excellent golfer and an all-star quarterback in high school. "I knew that Dale was

going to be a professional athlete of some sort because he had so much God-given talent," Ned says.

Ned thought that Dale's sport would be golf. Dale was the golfer of the year twice in his school district. The University of South Carolina offered him a **scholarship** to play that sport. They also wanted him to play football at their school.

Dale wasn't sure what he wanted to do with his life. He thought the university's offer was interesting.

Ned Jarrett was one of NASCAR's greatest early champions, winning 50 races.

"But racing was something that was in my blood," he told NASCAR.com. "I decided to work at the race track in Hickory for my dad. I knew right then that [racing] was what I was going to do."

Ned had retired from racing and ran the Hickory Motor Speedway. Dale helped out by doing everything from taking tickets to driving the **pace car.** It wasn't until 1977 that he first got behind the wheel of a race car at the track.

Today, more than 25 years later, there's a third generation of the Jarrett family racing cars. Dale's son and Ned's grandson, 26-year-old Jason Jarrett, was the **ARCA** Re/Max Series rookie of the year in 2001. He finished second in the overall standings. Those Jarretts just have to finish at the front.

A long way from Hickory: Ned (far left) and Dale Jarrett (center) started together in North Carolina and reached the top together in 1999.

ANOTHER KIND OF DRIVING

Dale says that if he had tried his hand at pro golf instead of auto racing, he'd probably be "starving" by now.

Don't bet on it. Despite the long NASCAR schedule, Dale remains an excellent and avid golfer. He has played well on some of the greatest courses in the world, including the Augusta National Golf Club and Pebble Beach.

"Golf gets me totally away from what I do," Dale told NASCAR.com. "It's quiet and away from everything. It also fuels that competitive fire inside me."

Jason Jarrett became a third-generation racer in the ARCA Series in 2001.

C H A P T E R   T W O

Sticking with It

Despite Dale's racing background, NASCAR success did not come easily—or quickly—for him. In 1982, he was one of the founding drivers of the Busch Series, a circuit one step below the Winston Cup Series. It wasn't until 1987, however, that Dale got a full-time ride on the NASCAR.

His first Winston Cup race came in 1984, when he placed 24th at Martinsville, Virginia. In three Winston Cup starts that year and another one in 1986, he earned less than $10,000.

"My racing career has been a struggle because I never had any money, so it has been one slow step at a time," Dale says.

He drove for various owners from 1987–1989 with little success. He finished in the top five in only two of 82 races.

While Dale often struggled to get his car to the track,
he sometimes also had trouble on it.

In 1990, Dale got the big break of his career. The Wood Brothers team asked him to fill in for an injured driver on their number 21 car.

Dale soon recorded his first victory, the 1991 Champion 400 at the Michigan International Speedway. He won in dramatic fashion. He and Davey Allison charged to the finish

Here Dale duels the great Richard Petty during Dale's first NASCAR victory in 1991.

ANOTHER FAMILY AFFAIR

Dale's first victory came in a battle with Davey Allison. Great driving is not all that Davey and Dale had in common. Like the Jarretts, the Allisons are another famous NASCAR family. While Ned Jarrett was a star in the 1960s, Bobby Allison was a top driver in the 1970s. Davey and Dale followed their dads to the track

and became rivals in the 1980s.

NASCAR has produced a large number of great racing families. On tracks in the 2002 season, fans could see Dale Earnhardt Jr., son of the legendary Dale Sr. Kyle Petty follows the tradition of his dad, Richard Petty. Richard is NASCAR's winningest driver of all time, with 200 victories.

There are brother combinations, too. Terry and Bobby Labonte have both been Winston Cup champions. Darrell and Michael Waltrip have each won many races. Geoff, Brett, and Todd Bodine form a unique triple play of brother drivers.

Though Ned has a new career as a broadcaster, he is always ready to help his racing son.

line side-by-side. Dale edged out his opponent by just 8 inches (20 centimeters).

"You dream about winning a race like that—racing door-to-door," Dale said afterward.

Ned Jarrett watched the race from a great seat. He was working for the television broadcast of the game. He was very pleased, of course, and fans watching on TV knew it! "I think I reacted pretty well," Ned told *USA Today*. "Then again, I don't know what I said. I'm sure I hollered because I was so excited."

The thrilling victory helped Dale finish 17th in the Winston Cup standings. He has not finished out of the top 20 since. Ned Jarrett thinks winning at Michigan was the turning point of his son's career. "That began to open some people's eyes," Ned says.

Dale was improving and becoming a good racer. In 1993, he took another giant leap forward at the Daytona 500, the biggest race on the NASCAR calendar.

C H A P T E R   T H R E E

The Super Bowl of NASCAR

—

Joe Gibbs coached the Washington Redskins to three Super Bowl titles. He used a different quarterback in each of those championship games. By 1992, Gibbs had left the NFL and was running a NASCAR team. The former football coach chose a "quarterback" to lead his racing team. That man was Dale Jarrett. Soon, the two combined to help Gibbs' car win the 1993 Daytona 500—the Super Bowl of NASCAR.

"What a great day!" Dale told NASCAR.com about his victory. "I knew once we got into the race that we had a good chance. I just needed to get myself into position because I had a great race car."

He was in position after 199 of the 200 **laps.** As the crowd screamed, Dale sped side-by-side next to the legendary Dale Earnhardt. Earnhardt tried furiously to pass Dale down the stretch. In the end, Jarrett won by less than a quarter of a second. "When you beat Dale Earnhardt at

Dale's team owner, Joe Gibbs (left), had already won one Daytona 500, in 1993 with Terry Labonte.

anything, you know you've accomplished something,"
Jarrett said after the race.

In 1963, Dale was standing on the **infield** watching his

dad in the Daytona 500. Ned held the lead on the last lap

In 1993, Dale's car was bright green. As he started
winning, he earned another kind of green—money!

before running out of gas and finishing third. In 1993, Ned Jarrett was working for television at the Daytona 500. On the air, he could not contain his excitement for his son at the finish.

Afterward, the son could not contain his excitement for his father. "This one was for my dad, for the whole family," Dale said.

By the end of that year, Dale had recorded 18 top-10 finishes. He also earned more than $1 million and finished fourth in the Winston Cup standings. It was by far the best finish of his career to that point.

"[Winning that race] did more for my career than anything else I've ever done," Dale says. Dale raced for Joe Gibbs' team through the 1994 season. Since 1995, Dale has been with a team led by owner Robert Yates.

Dale went on to win races in Charlotte in 1994 and Pocono in 1995. In 1996, another trip to Daytona again jump-started a great season in 1996. Dale's second Daytona

Dale salutes the track and his fans atop his No. 88 car after winning his first Daytona 500 in 1993.

500 victory came in the midst of NASCAR's boom in popularity in the 1990s. "What makes this [1996] win a little more special is knowing that so many people are coming over to the sport," Dale said afterward. "It's becoming their sport."

Those new fans had a new star to cheer. Jarrett won three more times in 1996. One of his wins came at the Indianapolis Motor Speedway in the Brickyard 400. He became become the first driver to win the Daytona 500 and the Brickyard 400 in the same year. He moved up to third in the final Winston Cup standings. In 1997, he won a career-best seven races. In 1998, he won three races and again finished third in the race for the Winston Cup. The young man who chose racing instead of golf had become one of the best drivers around.

Here's Dale in the lead during the 1997 season, the best of his career with seven victories.

FAMILY MATTERS

Dale dedicated his first Daytona 500 win to his dad. Ned and Martha Jarrett gave Dale a strong sense of family. Dale keeps that going in his own family. He and his wife Kelley and their three children still live in the town in which Dale grew up.

Dale and Kelley, who were married in 1984, live in Hickory, North Carolina, a town of about 35,000 people. They have three children: Natalee, Karsyn, and Zachary. Dale also has a son, Jason, from a previous marriage. He squeezes in as much time with them as he can between races of the hectic NASCAR season and during the off-season.

"I am fortunate that I'll have the chance to see Jason quite a bit because he's driving in the ARCA Series," Dale told *USA Today*. "But that off-season time with Zachary, Karsyn, and Natalee is precious."

Dale was joined by his wife Kelley (right) and their children after another victory in his revived career.

CHAPTER   FOUR

A Champion at Last

B y the late 1990s, Dale Jarrett had earned two Daytona 500 championships. He had a loyal fan following among fans. He had financial security . . . but he didn't have a Winston Cup championship. That all changed in 1999, when, at age 42, he became the oldest driver to win the championship for the first time.

Dale began the season with a disastrous 37th-place finish at the Daytona 500 that left him feeling down. Led by **crew chief** Todd Parrott, Dale's team regrouped and headed back to the track. "We never lost confidence," Parrott says.

One month after Daytona, Jarrett finished fifth at the Cracker Barrel 500 in Atlanta. His success there began a remarkable string of 19 consecutive top-10 finishes. The

streak vaulted him into contention for the Winston Cup title. He finished among the top five in 24 of the final 34 events. He won races at Richmond, Michigan, Daytona (the Pepsi 400), and Indianapolis. The late-season victories helped him capture the championship with ease.

"Perseverance pays off, along with hard work and dedication," Dale said in the *Fort Worth Star Telegram*. "I hope it'll be an inspiration to other drivers, owners, crew chiefs, and crew members alike. If you work hard and dedicate yourself to what you're doing, then you can become champions. You're never too old."

Jarrett proved his title was no fluke when he came back to win a pair of races in 2000, including his third Daytona

In 1999 (action above), Dale finally reached the top, winning the Winston Cup championship (right).

Winston Cup
NASCAR Winston Cup Series
1999 NASCAR WINSTON CUP CHAMPION
DALE JARRETT
ROBERT YATES RACING
NASCAR

It just kept getting better for the veteran driver in 2000, when he hoisted another Daytona 500 trophy.

500, and finish fourth in the points standings.

In 2001, Dale won three races in a four-week stretch early in the season to take the Winston Cup lead. He led the points standings midway through the year before finishing fifth. It was his sixth consecutive year in the top five. However, the second half of the 2001 season was marred by accidents at Pocono, Kansas City, and Talladega.

"I got beat up in a couple of accidents, and that made it difficult," he told NASCAR.com. Still, it only increased his resolve to come back stronger than ever. He wanted to "go back to winning races consistently and be in the top 10." High expectations are what you have when you've become one of NASCAR's biggest stars.

NASCAR drivers only drive 500 miles (805 kilometers) or so in each race. Dale Jarrett's road to the top has been much longer than that. "I believe that things are brought to you when you're ready for them," he says. "It's just taken me a long time to be ready for this."

MAN OF THE YEAR

Dale is not only a champion on the track, he's a champion off it, too. He's a two-time recipient of the NASCAR True Value Man of the Year Award. This award is given each year for involvement in civic and charitable activities.

"This is an award that can go to any driver, team owner, or sponsor who dedicates their time and effort to a lot of good causes," Dale said. "That's one thing that makes me extremely proud to be associated with NASCAR."

Dale is a national spokesman for the Disabled American Veterans and the Susan G. Komen Breast Cancer Research Foundation. Those who know him best say his work for charities is just an extension of himself.

"Dale is just a real good person, that's all there is to it," crew chief Todd Parrott told the *Boston Herald*. "He's a good family man. He's a good Christian. He's just a real good person."

For both his car's American flag paint job and his great racing career, fans and fellow drivers salute Dale Jarrett.

DALE JARRETT'S LIFE

1956   Born on November 26 in Conover, North Carolina

1977   Begins racing in the Limited Sportsman Division at Hickory (North Carolina) Motor Speedway

1982   Competes as a regular driver in the inaugural year of NASCAR's Busch Series circuit

1984   Finishes 14th in his first career Winston Cup race at Virginia's Martinsville Speedway

1984   Marries wife Kelley on June 22

1991   Earns his first victory in his 130th career start at the Champion 400 in Michigan

1992   Begins racing for the Joe Gibbs team

1993   Wins the prestigious Daytona 500 for the first time

1995   Joins the Robert Yates Racing team

1996   Becomes the first driver to win the Daytona 500 and the Brickyard 400 in the same year

1999   Wins his first Winston Cup championship

2000   Becomes only the fourth driver to win at least three Daytona 500s in his career

GLOSSARY

ARCA Re/Max Series—the racing events run by the Automobile Racing Club of America

crew chief—the "coach" of the race team, the person responsible for keeping things running smoothly before and during a race

infield—the portion of a racetrack inside the path formed by the road-way

laps—the word that describes the times a car goes completely around the track

NASCAR—the National Association for Stock Car Automobile Racing

pace car—the vehicle that drives ahead of the field in a race to get all the racers off to an even start. It pulls off the track when the checkered flag drops.

perseverance—an ability to stick to a task, in spite of obstacles

scholarship—an award for excellence in sports or academics that pays a student's college fees

Winston Cup—The Winston Cup championship is earned by accumulating the most points over NASCAR's grueling 38-race schedule each year.

The pace car (at the bottom right of photo) leads the field for a lap or two to get them up to speed.

FOR MORE INFORMATION ABOUT DALE JARRETT

Books

Dale Jarrett: Track Sounds. New York: Talking Pages, 1998.

Jarrett, Dale (editor). *Speedweeks: 10 Days at Daytona*. New York: Harper Entertainment, 2000.

Moriarty, Frank. *Dale Jarrett*. New York: Metro Books, 2000.

Poole, David. *Dale Jarrett: Son of Thunder*. Champaign, Ill.: Sports Publishing, Inc., 2000.

Web Sites

Dale Jarrett's Official Site
http://www.dalejarrett.com
For information on Dale's career, his family, and his racing team

NASCAR's Official Site
http://www.nascar.com
This site does an excellent job taking you through an entire season of NASCAR. It also has history of the sport, as well as a dictionary of racing terms.

Charlotte Observer Site
http://www.thatsracin.com
The web site for the *Charlotte* (North Carolina) *Observer* newspaper; a great site for fans to read about their favorite drivers

INDEX

ABOUT THE AUTHOR

Jim Gigliotti is a freelance writer who lives with his wife and two young children in Oak Park, California. He has worked for the University of Southern California athletic department, the Los Angeles Dodgers, and the National Football League.